JOHN HARE

A MOUTHFUL OF MINNOWS

To my dear uncle and mentor, Jim Lish

GREENWILLOW BOOKS
An Imprint of HarperCollinsPublishers

Alphonso loved to fish.
It was his very favorite thing to do.

One morning he set out to fish for some breakfast.
"Good luck!" said his friends.

Alphonso swam deep into the pond.

He tucked himself between some moss and an old tire, opened his mouth, and stayed perfectly still . . .

. . . except for his tongue. Alphonso had a special tongue
that looked like a yummy worm
if he wiggled it just right.

But fishing isn't easy, and not all fish would fall for his trick. Alphonso knew that a true angler had to be patient.

Sure enough, a little minnow approached.
"Mmm, a delicious worm!" said the minnow.

Such a small fish did not interest Alphonso.

Then the little minnow said, "This worm is so big that I'm going to get my friends so we can share it!"
And he swam away.

One tiny minnow isn't worth it, thought Alphonso.
But a few tiny minnows sounds like a delightful snack!

Soon the minnow returned with two friends.
They argued over who would get the first bite.

Why, that would be me! thought Alphonso.

But as Alphonso prepared to chomp down on his seafood snack, he heard one of the minnows say, "Wait . . . we shouldn't be selfish. Let's share this worm with the whole school!"

The minnows swam off.

Now we're talking breakfast!
thought Alphonso.

The minnows returned with their whole school.
They all crowded into Alphonso's mouth,
eager to take a bite of the worm.

And just as everyone was about to dig in,
one little fish said . . .

Hey, everyone! Maybe we should invite
Big Betty to take the first bite. She's big
and slow but doggone it, it's her birthday!"

The other minnows agreed, and off they swam.

Alphonso was getting very excited. I won't need to eat for days after this! he thought.

A while later, the whole school returned with Big Betty.
Alphonso waited for them to squeeze in around the worm.
As he waited, Big Betty began to speak. . . .

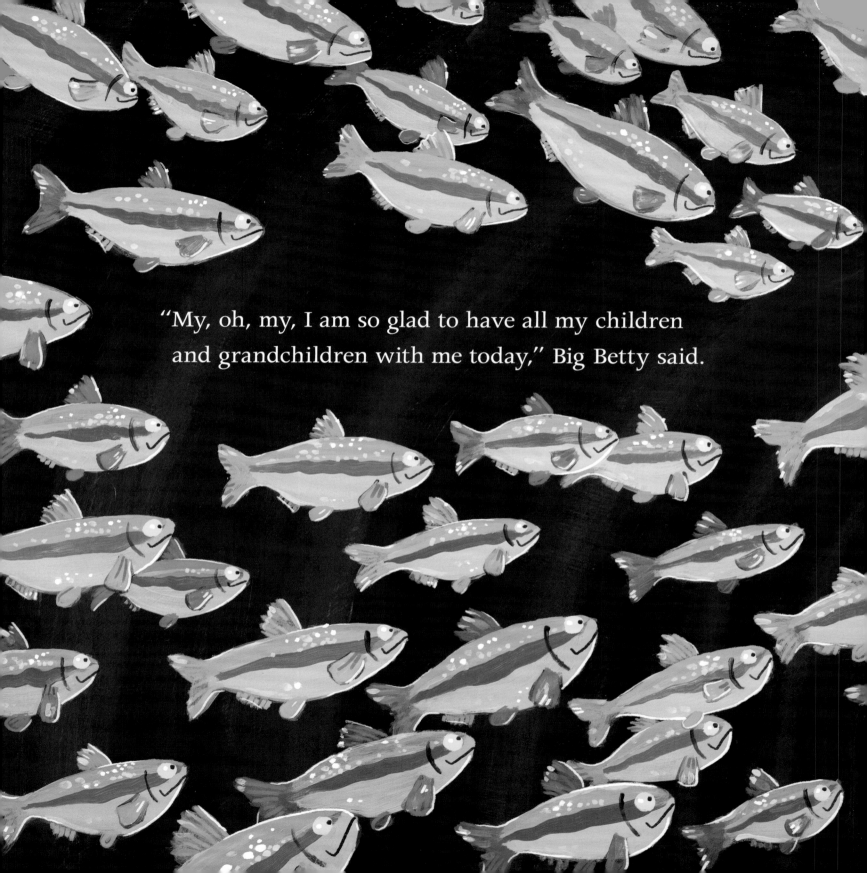

"My, oh, my, I am so glad to have all my children and grandchildren with me today," Big Betty said.

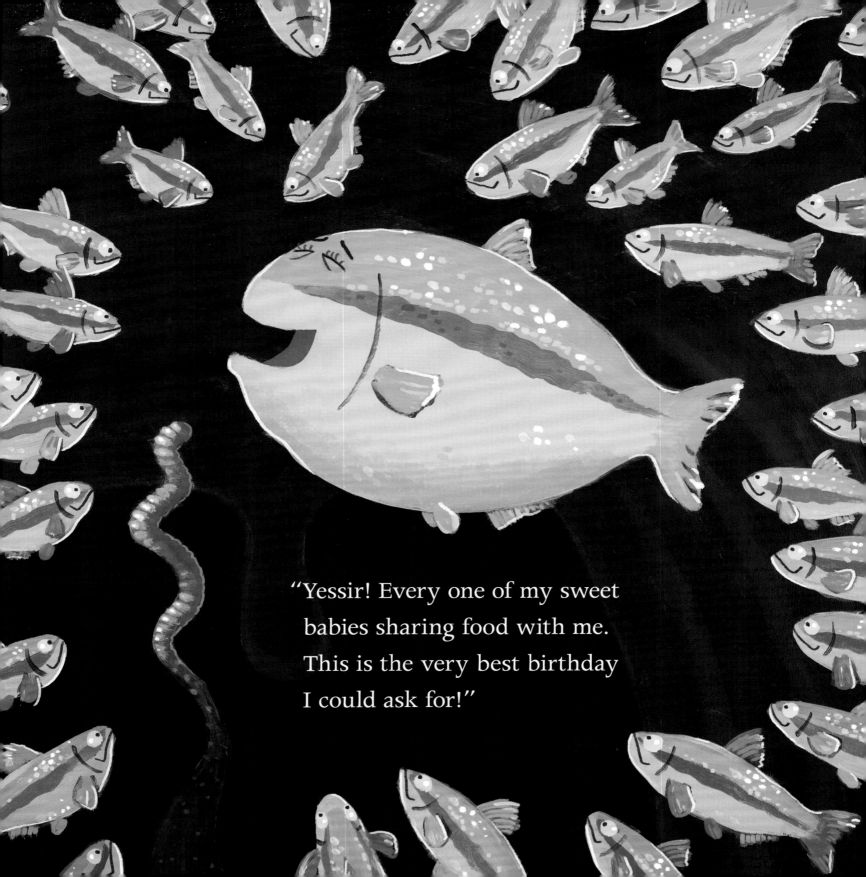

"Yessir! Every one of my sweet babies sharing food with me. This is the very best birthday I could ask for!"

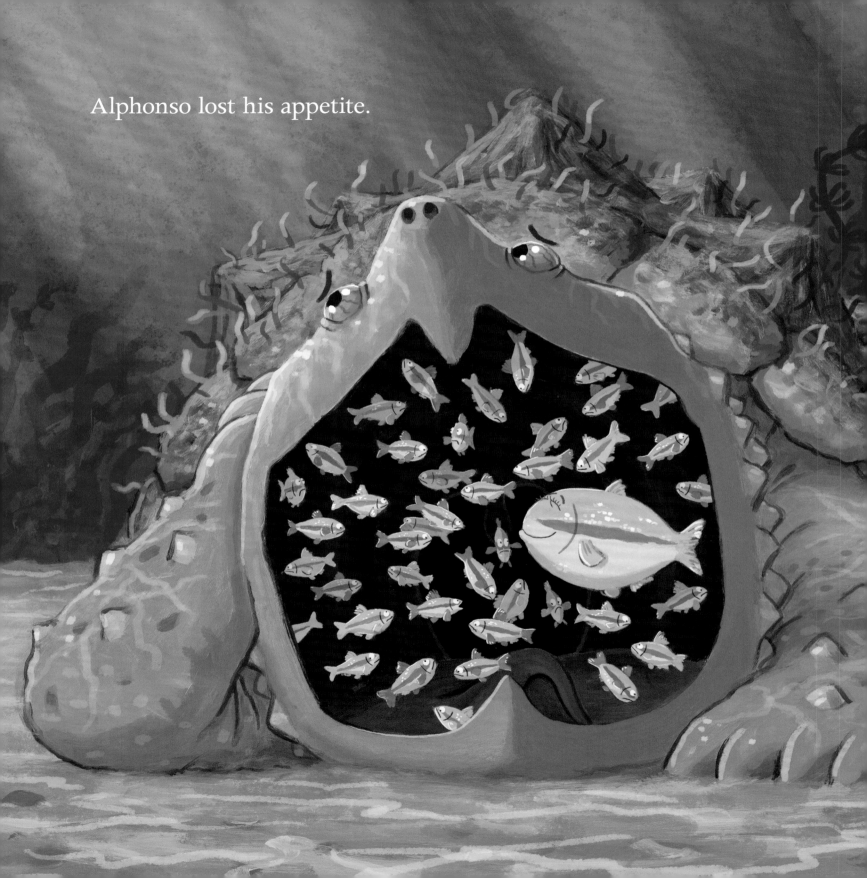

Alphonso lost his appetite.

"Big Betty! Big Betty!
The worm is gone!"
one of the little minnows cried.

"That's okay!" said Big Betty. "It's still a great day.
Let's go find something else to eat together."

Alphonso decided to head back to the surface of the pond.
"Who needs breakfast anyhow?" he mumbled.

But then he heard one of the minnows say, "Big Betty! Look! There's another big, juicy worm!"

"Big Betty! No!"
Alphonso shouted.

That morning,
Alphonso didn't catch anything,
but that was okay.

Because Alphonso's favorite part of fishing
is telling a new fish story to his friends.

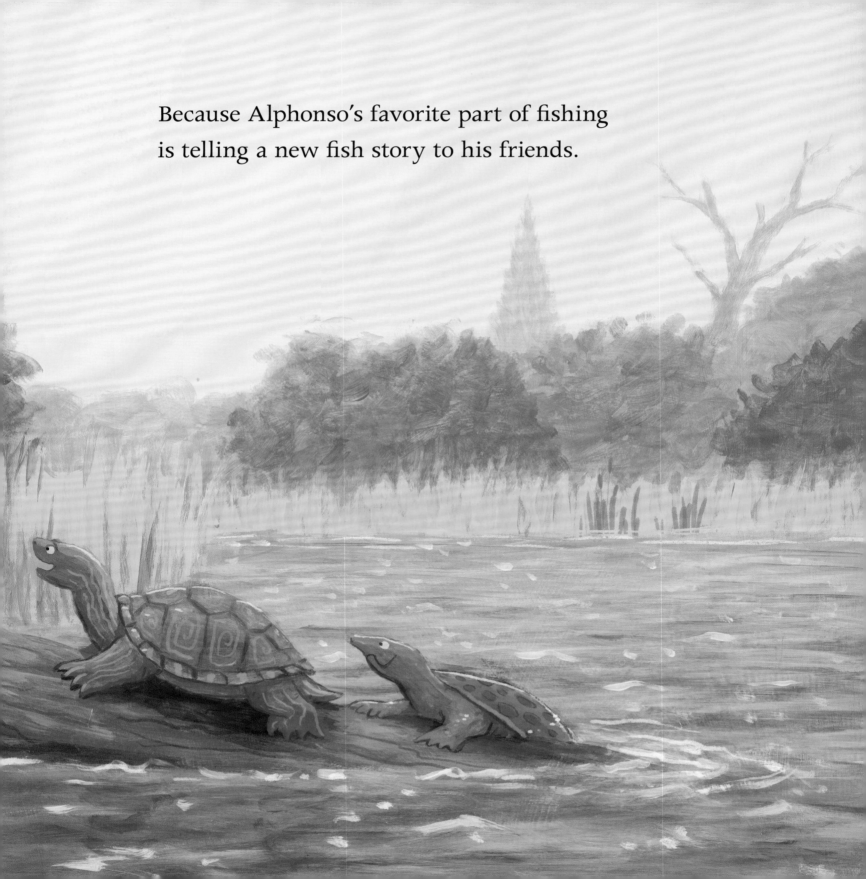

THE AMAZING ALLIGATOR SNAPPING TURTLE

There are two kinds of snapping turtles, the common snapping turtle and the alligator snapping turtle. The common snapping turtle has an oval-shaped head with eyes that are visible from above, a bumpy shell that gets smoother as they age, and a long sawtooth tail. The alligator snapping turtle has three obvious ridges running down the length of its shell. They also have a big, triangular-shaped head and a hooked beak.

COMMON SNAPPING TURTLE

ALLIGATOR SNAPPING TURTLE

Alligator snapping turtles are fishers! They find a spot underwater where they can sit motionless, open their mouth wide, and wiggle their pink, wormlike tongue to attract unsuspecting fish. Once a fish swims too close, the turtle's enormous mouth snaps shut.

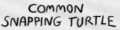
Hmmm

Alligator snapping turtles are among the biggest turtles. They can grow to have shells more than thirty inches long and can weigh more than two hundred pounds. That's a big turtle!

Snapping turtles often have fuzzy algae growing on their shells and head. It doesn't mean they're dirty, and it's not bad for them. In fact, the algae helps the turtles stay hidden while they wait for a yummy fish to wander by.

Snapping turtles aren't able to retreat into their shells like other turtles when they feel threatened. But with powerful legs, a strong neck, and a lightning-fast bite, they can defend themselves in the water or on land. But like most animals, they would rather avoid dangerous situations.

So, if you see a snapping turtle in the wild, leave it alone and let it do what it does best—catch fish and tell stories to its friends.

NOPE.